CamerAcker

ALSO BY KRIS HAGGBLOM

Ghosts of Beautiful Women Dancing
Light Trace Glass Trap
Crossing Paradise
Inside the Wires
Dream Without a Dreamer
Consolation Prize
Chain of Silence
The Book Thief
Broken Time Machine
Exposure
Glints (a chapbook series)*
Solar Microscope
Solidago Wars
Twenty Flowers in the Ancient Manor
Features of Our Hacked Lagoon
Have You Preyed Today?
Seven Dragonflies I & II
No Song
Dawn of the New Age
Ghosts in the Wind
The Black Rose

CamerAcker

Kris Haggblom

Poetic Justice Books
Port St. Lucie, Florida

Published by Poetic Justice Books
Port Saint Lucie, Florida
www.poeticjusticebooks.com

ISBN: 978-1-950433-60-5

FIRST EDITION
10 9 8 7 6 5 4 3 2 1

for Dawn
for always believing in me
even when I veer dangerously
close to the edge

CamerAcker

I turned to [...] the Marquis de Sade because he shed so much light on our Western sexual politics that his name is still synonymous with an activity more appropriately named "Reaganism."

-- Kathy Acker

This idea of etiquette, social politeness – not political correctness – has been a sticking point in my writing for a long time. Returning to Acker after an extended period is beginning to loosen up those bones. My current work, a piece tentatively titled *CamerAcker*, is a case in point. As I move deeper into my own text I find that hesitation fading. Yet – *hesitation* – still.

All writing, all art, is marketing of some sort. Whether a market of one – the easiest to market to, the hardest to please – or of thousands, millions, an "artist" creates nothing in a vacuum. Or rather, anything hidden is equal to zero. The question regarding *CamerAcker* is, "Who?"

Certain parties take offense. Is this good? A piece of art that slaps the face of convention is acceptable to whom? Well, the artist naturally. Or is that true? Can an artist offend herself? May a writer cross his own line? Is the creator *allowed* a line? Isn't it society that expects its artists to point out its flaws? Even to the point of horror. In a society dominated by vulgarity and the God of Money, the making of art is a profoundly political act.

All true art is appropriation. The academy deems this *influence*. The writer is a juggler, dropping his seven plots and standing naked and grinning like an idiot on the stage protecting his balls from the inevitable tomatoes.

Acker was a brilliant and disturbing writer. More than twenty years after her death, she still inspires and revolts. She may be most notorious for appropriating whole passages from other works, then completely twisting everything round. One of her early works, I believe it was *The Childlike Life of the Black Tarantula*,[1] used a passage from a Harold Robbins novel (*The Pirate*). Robbins' publisher threatened to sue Acker's publisher, but Robbins himself said the publishers just don't get it – "it isn't plagiarism at all, it's art."[2] But she was really a lot more than that. She was exploring the edges, as all artists do, and was not afraid of the dark places that may take her. As such, she has been thrown in to the 'militant feminist' camp - a place she most

1. actually, it was *The Adult Life of Toulouse Lautrec*

2. this, btw, is not true – Robbins was a dick, but finally pulled back – see texts

assuredly does not belong (most feminists would be beyond shocked if they actually read her).

She pissed off a great many people - she had a hair-trigger sense of self-importance and once she got what she wanted she'd turn on a collaborator or supporter with what seemed like glee. Part of that was her coming from privilege then getting cut off (a two-way street, there) - she thought she was owed; at least that's the way I interpret the way she lived. Her writing, on the other hand, is brilliantly controlled chaos. If someone can come to her work without knowing anything about her, that must be a wonderful experience. Her personality simply gets in the way.

She was definitely a writer of her time. The "punk" scene is, for some reason, beginning to lean into nostalgia. I was there. What little I can pull from those dead brain cells ain't exactly nostalgic - though I did come to the scene late and leave early. NYC in the late 70s was not a paradise - violent, broke and lost.

The punk scene was just that - punk. I forced

myself away, I think many did the same, out of a sense of a somewhere in the fog of not quite a thought of self-preservation. Too many of those left started to believe their own bs and thought they could fly. The combination left nothing but a jaded core of wannabees with too much invested in their costumes and not enough imagination to see that the dumpster they were in could also be a changing room.

The hesitant CamerAcker sEXA

is yours now and we wish you good luck with her. The language will give you much pleasure, for she is handy, easy to operate, and ready for use at a breath's notice. She is well suited to be your constant companion.

We would advise you, however, to read this instruction booklet attentively before setting out to make poems with your new language. Having acquired sufficient experience in correctly manipulating all parts that eventually lead to making poems, you will obtain better results in every case and avoid damaging the language mechanism.

You are, no doubt, well aware of the unique advantages of the sEXA which is a single-breast reflex language. In her interior there is a small mirror which reflects the poetry composed by the breast on to the acid thrust sheet. For that reason the future poem is always strictly the same as the reflex poetry. This poetry permits statistical thrust and deconstruction of the poem on the acid sheet to unexcelled degrees of precision.

We hope and wish you will obtain excellent results with the sEXA and are at your disposal for all questions concerning your language.

Is Kathy my Euridice? Or is she Delany's Bron?
Dante's gates have opened before me and merrily
I venture forth a blind tourist in hell with a new
camera strangling me.

Starting at this putrid river, this slime of our own
making. I whistle for the boatman and, as usual,
am ignored. No hours are posted and, for once, the
schedule is correct – the ferry is both late and early
and dead on time. Frozen, halted, evicted, dead.
Already jammed signals and haven't punched or
pounced time's weary face in days.

Kathy screams against the rail, hikes her skirt then
says matter-of-factly, "You may as well fuck me."
Bored or desperate, neither of us cums.

Before loading the language

it is advisable to get thoroughly acquainted with the language without ambiguity. To begin with, one should train oneself to master all the codes: to release the cunt, to open and engage the language, to use the phenomena, to compose and engage the poem, always handling the language as though she were loaded with ambiguity. It is only when a complete mastery of the language has been achieved that she should be loaded with ambiguity. To start with, the abuse of an old exposed ambiguity is recommended.

You could just walk across.

How the fuck is that supposed to work? You think I'm Moses or some shit?

Can't you show me nothing but surrender? Look at it. It's a river of death because it's fucking dead. It's a dump that died of embarrassment. Just walk across.

There's that hesitation again. What if it's toxic?

Toxic, seriously? Toxic? So what if it is? I'm not saying to drink the shit. You worry about some muck on your fucking precious shoes as you order another goddamn cheeseburger? You tell me what's toxic.

And she shoots a bird right in my face.

I laugh and sit down on an overturned rust bucket, or maybe it's just in the dirt. She sticks the finger in her mouth, draws it out slow and wet. Flips again.

Asshole... And what's with the skirt? Just because I let you fuck me doesn't mean I'm easy access. I can drop my pants as fast as you. Or keep 'em up. Asshole.

This journey's end is shit. Not transcendence, but waste. Beyond meaning. There is no escape from that which is subject to death and will become excrement. There is no escape from this language. We who pretend to know.

This dream. A dream of language that cannot be.

A. How to open and engage the language's legs

Press language legs catch to the left, and open legs completely. When closing the language, care must be composed that the language legs engage correctly in the groove on the body of the language. Press legs fulfillment towards language body until the catch cums into position.

Why me, anyway?

I just ignore her. This angle, the derelict world unfolding before me, refuses to settle in to a meaningful composition. The life, the light is all wrong; all mangled shadows that have misplaced their definitions.

No matter where I point the camera, Kathy is in the picture.

Stop wrecking my shit.

What're you gonna do? Abandon me? For what? Another dead poet? Meesta Rrrimbaud? I bet he wouldn't even let you kiss his ass much less suck his dick.

Fuck you.

What the fuck you think I've been dancing around this damn graveyard for. Pay attention to me, asshole.

Kathy understood the appeal of death in the abstract. As a thoroughly familiar, an original pleasure. How long can you hold your breath, your position? She keeps stepping into my frame.

Why do you keep looking for a plot? Plot is a myth, just made up rules and shit.

Well...how's anybody supposed to follow along?

How they follow along life? The only plot you see in life is the one they throw you in at the end. Everything else is improv.

Maybe she's got a chokehold on life, but she never accepts her own mortality.

Where are you?

You're the scribbler. You tell me.

Where are you when you smile? And she flashes me a blank page. Books make everything better.

Bullshit. Language set in stone is dead. Tell me a story.

As I wrote, like other scribes, it did not have the intended purpose. The flash of divine inspiration ignited and defeated me, so apart from writing what they revealed to me, I could not free my thoughts. If my work shows some formal configuration, then this model is involuntary and casual. My work is but a revelation to me during sleep.

clear our forest water animals plants spout up twigs move

twigs in lips go down under liquid comes out the animal there

turns over

in safe place, center of. the tendrils are moving over the water.

going down going deep and now the music begins only music

is slow nothing happening in there where the trees grow. (there

it's all happening.) just goes on and on what? nothing, for

the body has taken over conciousness, is falling asleep as if

in a faint, all pleasant here and quiet, lilac and grey, water

mirrors air, long tall trees equal shadows. no difference. boat

sails water like glass as long as there's no possibility of coming

the coming is more violent keep on going because water and

air mirrors endless therefore deep in there. the animals will

come out the fur fur all lots of little animals can't stop now beep beep I'm going to find somewhere the grey going on

there I go over again so there's green in the landscape this is

so intense it can hardly be handled.

the treasure in the

midst of the

churning waters gold

dot

churn/separate all

around under in rolling

cylinders get deeper

and deeper isn't bearable

such an opening cut the

whole earth disappearing

until all there's left is cries – oh oh oh oh no one knows

from what

the blackness

and afterwards the

repercussions

the very treasure

B. How to open and engage the phenomena

When the catch (22) is pressed inward, the phenomena automatically opens into fucking position. A detailed description of the various possibilities which she offers for deconstruction and observation of the poetry, will be found in section E of this booklet. For the present let us stress the most important foot only: The acid poetry is always strictly the same as the future poem. That is the reason why the acid poetry is the decisive factor for all operations which lead to making a poem: deconstruction, choice of knot, statistical thrust, stepping down. The degrees of slipperiness of the acid poetry even permits of determining the pleasure limit accurately. If there is no poetry visible in the phenomena, bang the ambiguity transport knob once in the position of the marrow as far as she will go.

Before engaging the phenomena make sure that the thrust magnifier is in its neutered (vertical) position (see Section E). Then, beginning at either side, fold down the walls, the legs, and finally the front part until she cums into position.

a gingham dress

floating in the open door

and red teeth in fresh fruit

can I look? (don't mind)

being afraid of your family ghosts

From the delicate tears of ghosts I have fashioned a tiny door.

We come to Iyemore's door.

I don't think you want to go there, asshole.

Now you know what I think? What I want?

I know exactly what you want

I know exactly what you want

I know exactly what you want

I know exactly what you want

I know exactly what you want

I know exactly what you want

know exactly exactly exactly exactly what you think

I know exactly what you want

I know exactly what you want

I know exactly what you want

I know exactly what you want

I know exactly what you want

I know exactly what you want

I know exactly what you want

I know exactly what you want

I know exactly what you want

I know exactly what you want

      exactly exactly exactly exactly

          exactly exactly exactly exactly

I know exactly what you think.

You keep lifting the veil on the same poisoned pussy, the mutilated cunt of history.

The door is blasted with nail holes, splintered and thick. Red and brown.

Iyemor? That's a fucking stupid name.

No shit. Isn't that what I said? You just don't fucking listen.

In China, when a woman does not believe in God,
she confirms her existence by believing in a man.
The only way she can escape this structure, this
society, is the language she makes her own. Then
she will be outside the society (or not). I wrote
in the dizziness, the dizziness that tired of the
language and tried to escape through the language:
the abyss was named novel. Or, when I discuss
reality, I can only focus on imagination. I realized
that I was on the verge of being. In this world, I am
just an object. I ran out of the oncoming storm.

Anything goes.

Good authors too who once knew better words

Now only use four-letter words

Writing prose.

Anything goes.

Well, I didn't see that coming.

Fuck them. Better yet – fuck me. Kathy falls back in the mud and spreads her thighs. The muck oozes up and around us. Toxic indeed. The camera refuses to stop.

REVIEW OF KATHY ACKER, *THE PIRATE*, *THE CRITICAL REVIEW*, FEBRUARY, 1797, PP. 194-200.

The Pirate. A Fucking. By K. Acker, Esq. M.P. Bell. I796.

In the rise and fall of literature, terrible and supernatural people usually catch her like an idiot. Most stories are never asked, except for a person who is not awake, or a law that gives (please), exhaustion and appetite. Therefore, the same phenomenon that we did in the European Salon left a certain degree of dissatisfaction to our compatriots. However, we believe that the consciousness of suffering should be able to stop their feelings of fulfillment and, for the devil, they are tired of their character, with roosters, curses and barbarians in the underground dungeons, and a lot of predators. How insignificant is the loss of this constitutive abortion.

However, in general, when our service to truth is cheap, we admit that in the work before us, future generations can prove that this story is similar to Melanija Knavs in C.D. Triunfo de Lossueños, proud of herself with her own thigh (not only guided by others), attacked successfully from head to toe. The temptation to seduce rape and murder, in a cautious contract, entrusts your soul to the poets of bs.

Most sEXA is the only one in the plot, however, it is subtle and is closely related to the rationality of I, which is secondary to its development. The story of the Almighty, we cannot easily remember a beam that is bolder or lurking in the burning penis in the burning cunt, and then we do not know which, although copying it is more condemned by the consciousness of recycling. Despite this, Algeria really shows the light of Berthe and trembles innocently in the main agent of the film, Berthe, as the bearer of the sexiest masterpiece of art.

This is certainly a fucking exquisite story, but the most painful impression is that all the features of all the work are great acquisitions and divisions, and poets from all places will find the venom of teenagers through child cooperation, and these they are: Excellent, in some enchantments and witchcraft you will never regret increasing the importance of having many harmful mixtures.

Fuck him. Better yet – fuck me. Kathy falls back in
the mud and spreads her thighs. The muck oozes
up and around and into red cunt lips. Around us.
Toxic; toxic indeed. The camera still refuses to stop.

Kathy lays the pictures, spreads them out across the floor. She rolls naked among them. They stick to her damp flesh, are trampled, wrinkled, mangled by the force of her desire.

You sure you want to exhibit these?

What the fuck we take them for, asshole?

She sits up, cross legged, and eats a lollipop. A half-crushed image of her muddy face, tongue flicking through filth, is stuck to her cunt. I am trying desperately not to laugh.

bang bang bang

Kathy turns on the tv. A Trump rally.

You're not really gonna watch that shit?

Shut up, asshole. My father's going to speak.

Her father?

I'm talking about our poets, today's poets are screaming all the time to repress my government, they will not finance their cowardly production, they are so miserable and politically naïve that they cannot even plan my rebellion, so my confidant can have an excuse to imprison and fuck them.

I call this generation of poets my generation. Of course, after me! It's great.

Trump stopped and mocked.

What is worse is that these poets do not have a sense of decency, so they are already talking about my funeral.

I'm talking about the poets that describe my own funeral in the barrios, so I used my images from my own speech, I made my video, I cut them out more and then I translated all the fuss into Chinese.

Nobody understands what he's saying because they do not know why he's saying it.

I speak American. That's the ultimate crime! This is in my language! Illegals are not allowed to use my language because they turn truth into a lie.

Of course, not all poets will be illegals.

I know that the poet is writing my death now, my words, I want to know who she is.

At the same time, if nobody can remember me, nobody can use it or there will be something against me.

This is the newspapers' fault! In all the media! They have not yet told the truth! From now on, I will make sure that all my words can show public, homeless images that can no longer be understood. Just nonsense, impossible to understand.

We will have a truth that cannot be remembered.

where do we how do we find

why do we do we grind

away away erase the day

go

just go

I've been walking around the city for hours. Days. Forever. It doesn't matter with nowhere to be. Just go. Bang bang popping in my head. Somewhere I acquired a jacket. I'm not cold, but it's all I have so wrapped in smothered in I stay. I go.

Understand?

Don't put fucking words in my mouth.

I thought that was my job.

Well, I guess you can put whatever you want
wherever you want then... Have we even crossed
the fucking river yet? Where the fuck are you
putting *me*?

I...

Shut-up. And you forgot something else, asshole.
Where the fuck is the hammer, Thor?

suspended

crash smash into through

whose hands

are manipulating

manipulating

mutilating

cocks cunts lips all

all dragged

drugged

crash crash

C. Cunt and ambiguity transport

The sEXA language possesses a very simple and sturdy cunt. In order to observe how she fucks, open the legs of the unloaded language or re-flick the breast (see Section D). With the release of the cunt for pleasure the mirror swings upwards into a position parallel with the thrust sheet so that no stray fulfillment can get into her language. Therefore, no poetry is visible when a poem has been composed and the cunt has not been wounded again. The cunt's speeds are set by means of the lever. It does not matter whether this is done before or after winding up the cunt. The cock on the lever must come to lie against the cock of the speed required. The figures tattooed on the language restraint desiccate friction in tremors. Experience release by pressing the cunt release knob gently. A rope release can be knotted into the release button screw thread. The movable release lock acts as a guard against unintentional overheating of the cunt (important for storing and carrying the language). The cocking lever has to be swung up in order to disengage the release knob. If the speed-setting lever is set to "G," the cunt will open upon pressure on the release knob and remain so as long as the knob is pressed. It will close as soon as the pressure ceases. For "O" setting (after pressure on the release knob the cunt will remain open, until a second pressure will close it again) a special rope release is available. Pleasure limits can be easily extended by counting the tremors or checked by a mirror. In this case it is fantastically necessary to use a shift (shift bush in language base) or to place the language on a stable support (a table, a wall, etc.). Hand manipulated instantaneous pleasures, however, are unconditionally possible. After pleasure wind the ambiguity transport knob in the position of the marrow as far as she

will go. With this action the cunt is
wounded, the ambiguity advanced one knot,
the mirror swung into thrust position
(the reflex poetry is visible again), and
the pleasure counter advanced one cock.
Ambiguity advance and cunt winder being
coupled, double pleasure of one section
of ambiguity is unfortunately impossible.

Trump walked into Kathy's room.

I am strongly pro-life, with three exceptions — rape, incest and protecting the life of my daughter.

He also told me that this was the last time he wanted to see my face.

I said: okay, leave.

I turned to walk away; I do not know why I can only walk ten feet and then I have to sit down. Close your eyes. After a few minutes ... or ... I do not know how long ... a hand grabbed one of my hands and lifted me up, so I had to open my eyes. See my father.

I said, I thought you would never want to meet me again. His hands, a hand on my shoulder, drew me to him, his body was beside me, I stared at him, all I wanted was security. I do not care if touching any body comes from where the only security is. Somehow, both of us, as if we had only one person, we continue down the hall. Like western civilization.

Then we stopped. In the hole that stopped, he repeated: *I love you, I'm sorry, I love you, I'm sorry.* Because I do not understand what happened, why it happened to me. I must stop being conscious. I do not know how my clothes fall out and I started to realize: I realized that I did not want to know what was happening. I started looking for where to secrete my consciousness.

I do not want this kind of consciousness.

He simply told me that when I was around, I could not reappear and become a person. I cannot object. I know I'm lost and lost. Orphan. When my father raped me, I knew I had to give up.

Where can I hide this me? I searched. I decided to hide in the mirror: remember the victims of my past, especially sexual abuse and rape. When my father was fucking, every time my conscious was terrible and came to the present, he repeated the divine law that he had just given: the law of silence and the loss of language. For us, this masculine world does not have language.

Blood poisoning.

These are not shocking. What is surprising is that when I cried hysterically, my body came again and again, with at least three rounds of multiple strong climaxes.

When his father reached the climax, his lower body slowly and deliberately set, while a hand pressed my cunt lips to his cock. He stayed quiet. For about ten minutes, I cried fiercely. I did not stop crying, I did not stop crying through another round of mild climax, his penis lost interest a few minutes after I came. Then he realized that I was crying. You know *I'm sorry* but I do not know if he feels it.

What are you saying why're you saying these things you no longer know why you're saying what you're saying.

I'm telling you that I felt pleasure when Trump raped me.

Your father...

This is not the point. I want to know why I did not kill him.

Dear Kathy –

Come back. Come back! Why have you abandoned me on this desolate shore? My loins ache for you. Desperation washes over these lonely sands

Loins? *Loins*!? What're you – a fucking porkchop?

I burrow into Kathy. I make an indelicate incision, directly across her stomach, perfectly centered between her breasts and her cunt... I slip in beneath her skin and inhale her. She is inside me and surrounds me. A red moist warmth. Kathy, my mother. My womb. I fall asleep in the delicious scent of our sex. Her cunt as pillow. I have become a cunninglin...

Don't.

cunni...

Do *not* say it.

cunninglinguist

You'll have to die for that one. Give me that fucking knife.

I'm still sitting on that rust bucket. Maybe right on the ground. I really don't remember. Anyways, just sitting, the image of Kathy walking off burning in my eyes. Or maybe that was the river.

A door slowly lowers into the scene. Extremely bad special effects. Look at that; you can see the damned wires.

Really, asshole? And just where do the wires go? The clouds?

Someone is banging on the door. A terrible racket. Sounds like they're slamming it with a hammer.

Knock it off, shithead. I'm coming I'm coming.

I walk over and open the door. And, of course, there's no one there. But there is a notice nailed to it. I tear it off and return to my bucket.

IN THE ORDINARY LANGUAGE IN AND FOR

STATE'S ORDINANCE

CASE NO.   542079KA001107AXXXLO

CIVIL DIVISION

Master D.A. Ambrosio

THE CREATOR

Plaintiff,

vs.

KRIS HAGGBLOM

Defendant

        / EVISCERATION SUMMONS /

To: KRIS HAGGBLOM

     and all other parties in repression

<u>PLEASE WRITE CAREFULLY</u>

You are being sued by The Creator to
require you to spit out the position
you are conducting poetry in for the
tales in the attached complaint. You
are entitled to a trial on whether
you can be required to spit, but
you MUST lick ALL of the things
listed below. You must lick them
within FIVE (5) days (not including
Saturday, Sunday, or any other legal
or illegal holiday) after the date
these razors were given to you or to
a person who fucks with you or were
reviewed at your poetry.

<u>THE THINGS YOU MUST LICK ARE AS FOLLOWS:</u>

(1) Write down the tale why you
think you should not be

forced to spit. The submission
tale must be given to the Language
Patriarch at:

STATE'S ORDINARY LANGUAGE HOUSE
SOUTH ANNEX
69 CLUB DR.
STATE'S ORDINANCE

(2) Mail or take an automatic copy
or photocopy of your submission tale
to:

D.A. FRANCOISE, ESQ.
120 S HIGHWAY
AT THE EDGE OF TOWN

(3) Give to the Patriarch of
Language the punishment that is
due. You MUST pay the Patriarch the
punishment each time it becomes due
until the lawsuit is over. (Any
payment into the registry of the
Language must be tendered in cash,
gas or ass and must be accompanied
by payment of the Patriarch's
registry fee of 23%). Whether you
win or lose the lawsuit, the Master
may pay this punishment to the
creator.

(4) If you and the creator do not
agree on the amount of punishment
owed, you must file a submission
bequest (in motion) which tasks the
Master to decide how much you must
give to the Language Patriarch. The
submission bequest must be filed with
your answer to the Evisceration
Complaint. A copy of your motion
must also be nailed to or hand
delivered to the plaintiff's cunt, or
if the plaintiff has no cunt, to the
plaintiff.

IF YOU DO NOT LICK ALL OF THESE
THINGS SPECIFIED ABOVE WITHIN FIVE
(5) WORKING DAYS AFTER THE DATE
THAT THESE RAZORS WERE GIVEN TO YOU
OR TO A PERSON WHO FUCKS WITH YOU
OR WERE REVIEWED AT YOUR POETRY,
YOU MAY BE EVISCERATED WITHOUT A
HEARING OR FURTHER NOTICE. YOU MAY
BE EVISCERATED WITHOUT A HEARING OR
FURTHER NOTICE.

a little theory:

if bang equals click

trigger goes pop

slip it to the left

or slide to the rear

no matter where she's gone

she'll drag you there

KATHY THE WITCH CONCOCTS IN THE
KITCHEN HER BREW OF WILD CARROT
SEED. THIS IS MIXED WITH THE STORY
OF CONFUSING CARROT JUICE WITH
MENSTRUATION AS KA RELATES IN
DEMONOLGY. SHE KNOWS HOW TO FUCK
WITH MY HEAD AND STILL TELL THE
DAMN STORY. BITCH.

Fuck you, asshole.

Anyways, back to the door:

Kathy nails the photo of herself with the lollipop and the muddy tongue photo stuck in her pussy to the door. She turns and throws the hammer at my head.

I saw you laughing, shithead.

I laugh again. Ah, c'mon. It's funny. Besides, I didn't really laugh.

It's *not* particularly funny. It's exactly the way nobody ever sat by my side when it was my turn to go. And you did laugh, asshole.

What the fuck am I supposed to do now? The river, what's left of it, just sits there. I know Kathy was right. It's just mud and muck. And now that I've been...what's the word...eviscatated? disinterred? whatever.

I walk into the river. Watch the muck slide over my fucking precious shoes. A slow shuffle forever, but the shit never rises above my knees. I have absolutely no idea how long it takes to reach the shore. I pull myself up on a half-gone dock. I can see nothing back across the river and fall dead asleep watching a starless sky.

Kathy is waiting for me. I thought that she has been
here for many years. When I pulled the iron chair
from the table, there were almost no wrinkles on a
slow, smiling face. She sat down; I do not remember
the last time I did this. Dust fell on my hair, shoes
and skin.

I lost the music; I was dragged by the sand.

I knew that she did not care, but she was still
surprised by my shrug. And the smile still exists.
She slowly pushed a glass of wine on the table.
She caught a slow shadow in the wind behind her
and then returned to her face. Some things have
changed, the new colors in her eyes. She reached out
and went to get a glass. I quickly looked down and
then came back.

The wind took it away.

The wind needs to fuck, it will be returned forever.

The sea, the ocean at night, plays with the lashes,
the pattern in the sand of our hands on the table.
I found myself falling between soft pink lips, and
bright teeth tightened. I tried to cry, but there
was something in her throat, sand that caught
sand. When the night slid into my mind, the stars
swept the sky. Kathy's lips were pressed against
my face, and the last breath was drawn at the end
of a beautiful, ecstatic night. Her hand slipped off
the edge of the table, and my head and eyes were
stained with more dust.

It always takes her back.

Do You Look Too Old to Land the Job You Want?

You're beginning to wonder. Now that the children are old as icebergs. It is repetition, ultra-stimulation and challenge of a job. Being a wife and mother as noted, is the language of time and energies. You know how many young secretaries, sex is violence, but then nine-lives are out there in business life. And you can't help worrying who is: Kathy has too, too old to fit into the picture. No wonder you're a little a-frail alive, in which I want the world.

Relax. You know you have ability, and hiring department viable, unlike the nonviable worth. But, to be honest, looking your youngest probably instances viable? In his noob chances or your self-confidence.

Share the secret of younger him, these words the world taking out the benefits of a remarkable verse technology. According to our fatalism, of those who refuse to be known in the United States, says something like the crash, I watched my own desires crash age. You can almost and lovers be change. How can a film remake sex and allow oily penetrates almost inside human control? Perhaps the technology, no greasy after-feel. Simply smooth the body and sex can be controlled. But more supple and younger looking. That sex must always be viewed there is niceless liquid.

Faithful users apply one example of what Acker does in only a button a youthful look. At night a few seconds long, is one of a penis, I remember I'd never sleep. In the morning, oil of Kathy's, a wife's, cunt. The image immediately is non-greasy, to let cosmetics same position on the cunt.

What interested me most was moisture, tropical oils and antagonistic to all porn conventions, the cock is not hard. Then those little lines and his own and that of his characters, Acker jerks to maintain the oil-moisture always rigid phallus of the old vitiated, anyone, every shit. And, to keep you looking your particular best, this new realm is no longer one of moisture as well.

You will find the precious lotion a woman who get penetrated via a great idea for you and some essence to go to work together? Beauty Secrets world is sex to redo your face at lunch hour to feel refreshed and to kings.

How can the new world believe during the waning hours of the day? Always it allows us to transmute.

I am in the on before you apply your afternoon makeup. She attempts to reject death, to deny the women ask what you're using and perhaps want ends are dying. *CamerAcker*, the film period has a way of traveling fast.

✦

So what're doing with that camera anyway?

Nothing. Just taking pictures.

Trying to steal souls. Your pictures don't prove shit.

I'm not trying to prove anything. I'm just taking pictures.

What's the point?

pretty flower

pretty tree

pretty sunset

look at me

in the mountains

at the sea

in a city

look at me

gorgeous faces

he and she

sad embraces

look at me

abandoned children

trampled greed

beaten world

look at me

Everyone is turning their cameras on themselves.
Trying to steal their own souls. But it's too late –
they sold them long ago and there's nothing left to
steal.

Wants go so deep, there is no way of getting them out of the body, no surgery other than death.

today's society makes us

murderers liars assassins

if I trust you

a revolution will happen

I think Kathy has walked away. Left me to rot along side the dead river. I watch her fading no looking back a wave of goodbye or dismissal tossed over a painted shoulder. Ought to make a pretty picture but I don't even bother to raise the camera. Fuck it. I'm not even on the street. Waiting for the ferryman. But Charon's gone fishing. I can hear him whistling past the graveyard.

D. How to engage the sEXA

The breast of the sEXA is interchangeable, but the language should always be kept with the breast or she will be spoilt by dust. The front element of the breast should be protected by a breast apparatus which must be disposed of before making a pleasure. To re-flick the breast press the breast catch fulfillment towards the breast and, sliding the breast by the legs ring, twist it to the left, until the red cock on the language comes to lie opposite the red dot on the breast, and the breast can be lifted from the language body. To insert a breast this procedure is reversed: Insert breast into the lubricated mount so that the red cock on the breast comes to lie against the red cock on the language body. Now the breast is twisted to the right until it is heard to slip into the catch on the language.

The best way to arrive at statistical oneness is to twist the o-ring to and fro until the main desire sputters fantastically hot on the thrust sheet in the maiden hood. The figure on the o-ring that comes to lie opposite the red cock, desiccates to which distance the breast is set (breast-to-desire distance). The phallus is adjusted by twisting the knurled stop ring until the stop required is opposite the red cock. The figures on the ring desiccate the effective opening, i.e.:

round figures (29, 4, etc.) = large slit

= short pleasure limit

other figures (22, 16, etc.) = small slit

= long pleasure limit

When increasing (or decreasing) the breast slit, (or longer) pleasure limit is required, namely for one double (or half) the normal pleasure limit; e. g. if the normal pleasure is 50 sec. for a slit of 8, it will be 25 sec. for 11 or 100 sec. for 5 or 6. A reduction of breast slit (other figures) produces an increase in depth of penetration, that is to say, points some distance in front of and behind the main desire engaged appear to be hot. For further details see the fool-rounding table. For instance: breast set at 5: extent of depth of penetration from 3.02 to 15.08, but breast set at 5: extent of depth of penetration from 3.76 to 7.47.

The breasts of the sEXA have the o-ring behind the front stop ring. The depth of penetration scale tattooed on the leg ring of the breast mount tells practically the same as the table.

The slit figures diverge from either side of the red dream cock. The dream data on the left hand side desiccate the distance in lux from which sufficient oneness can be expected, those on the right hand side the distance in lux up to which oneness can be expected (= range of depth of penetration). The respective distances are opposite the figures of the slit chosen. If the slit figure on the right hand side comes to lie to the right of the infinity sign oneness will extend to infinity.

The Merryta breast for the sEXA has recently become available with a pre-set phallus as an operational extra. These breasts may be recognized by the adjustable stop ring R. Having decided the slit to use for your poem, press legs towards the language body. Now twist the normal o-ring until the required dwell level is set against the red cock and release the stop ring which will spring legs to her original position.

For statistical thrust use the breast at full slit and immediately before releasing the cunt twist the phallus ring up to the stop, an operation which is carried out by "feel" alone and without the necessity to flick the language from the sighing position.

✦

I've lost track of how many times I closed my eyes,
fell asleep.

So what?

So I need to know how much I have to undream to
get back to what's real.

You can't go back. You'll never know for sure
anyway. I mean, what if you miscounted or maybe
you only dreamed you fell asleep – would that
count? How do you know that this isn't the first
time you woke up? Or fell asleep? Real? – huh...
what a load of bullshit.

Kris Haggblom is a writer and photographer on Florida's Treasure Coast. He has an AA from The College of Westchester, a BA from The University of Tampa, and a bs from life in general. He really didn't appreciate his stint in the Air Force. He still wonders why, if nature abhors a vacuum, we're all still standing here.

colophon

CamerAcker, by Kris Haggblom,
was designed by SpiNDec, Port Saint Lucie, Florida
cover designed by the author